# Gary's Prayer

**Written by Jonathan Johnson**

**Illustrated by David Boyce**

This story is dedicated
to Trey and Landon.

# Gary's Prayer

Written by Jonathan Johnson
Illustrated by David Boyce

"Learning to pray can indeed be a challenging task, but the more that you do it, the easier it becomes." Gary had become use to his parents praying in the morning time before he went to school. Since turning eight years old, Gary wanted to learn to pray for himself. But Gary had no idea how to start a prayer. So, Gary went to his parents for advice on how to pray. He asked them if they could teach him how to pray. His parents said, "Of course we will teach you to pray." Gary was nervous about learning to pray because he wasn't sure what to pray for or how to really pray at all.

Gary's parents suggested that he start off with a short prayer each morning. Gary's father sat him down and told him about a prayer that his parents taught him at a young age. The prayer was simple, but impactful. Gary's father explained that he was around the same age when he learned to pray, and that with practice, patience, and God's guidance, each prayer that Gary prays will be heard by the Lord.

As Gary and his father sat in the car, his father told him the prayer. "Angel's east angels west, Lord bless me to do my best. Amen." Gary's father asked him to repeat the prayer as practice. Not only did he repeat the prayer, but also understood to close his eyes and to bow his head as he prayed. After Gary prayed, his father gave him a hug and a hi-five. Gary's father explained that  God hears the prayers of a young child and to never be discouraged to pray.

Gary's father went on to explain the prayer that he taught Gary so that he would understand what the prayer meant. "When you ask God to allow you to do your best, He will give you what you ask for," Gary's father explained. "Be it on a test, a basketball game, or even learning something new, when you ask God to bless you to do your best, He will indeed bless you." Gary had a much better understanding of what the prayer meant, but was still confused on the angels east and angels west part of the prayer. His father told him that east and west simply meant that wherever you go, God will cover you from one end of the earth to the other.

After Gary was dropped off at school, he went in excited about the new prayer that he had just learned and told his friends what his father had taught him. The last thing that his father told him before he got out of the car was to, "Spread the good word of God. You might just turn a friend to God." Gary wanted to do his part in telling his friends about God. With learning that one prayer, Gary wanted to learn more about prayer as well as learn how to pray for other things.

When school was over for the day, Gary's mother picked him up. She asked how his day was, he responded by telling her that his day was great. His mother asked him what made his day so great. Gary told his mother about his school day, but also told her about the prayer that his father had taught him that morning. His mother was happy to see Gary so excited to learn about prayer. She asked him to recite the prayer that his father had taught him. Gary proudly repeated the prayer, "Angels east, angels west, Lord bless me to do my best. Amen." His mother smiled and told him how proud she was of him remembering the prayer. Gary's mother saw this as an opportunity to teach him another prayer. She would always bring Gary a snack when she picked him up from school. She told him, "It's one thing to pray in the morning, but you have to pray over your food as well." Gary was intrigued by what his mother had just said. He asked her why he needs to pray over his food. She explained that if it wasn't for God, we wouldn't have food to eat, so in all things be grateful for what you have.

Gary then asked, "How do I pray for my food?" His mother told him to bow his head and repeat after her. "God is grace, God is good, let us thank Him for our food. In Jesus' name, amen." The prayer that he had just repeated was totally different from the prayers that he was used to hearing his parents pray. His parents' prayers were a bit longer when they prayed in the morning and when it was time to eat. Gary's mother explained to him that the older you get, the more mature your prayers become.

As dinner time arrived, Gary and his parents sat down to eat. Normally, Gary's father would pray but this time, Gary offered to lead in prayer over the dinner. And he recited the prayer he had learned perfectly, "God is grace, God is good, let us thank Him for our food. In Jesus' name, amen. After dinner, Gary had to take his bath and get ready for bed. He had learned two new prayers, but still wanted to learn more.

His parents would tell him that it was important to pray each night before going to bed. Gary's parents did their best to pray over him each night before he went to sleep; but on this particular night, Gary wanted to pray himself. Gary's parents sat down with him to teach him one last prayer. And that prayer was, "Now I lay me down to sleep, I pray to the Lord my soul to keep. If I should die before I wake, I pray to the Lord, my soul He will take." Before Gary could recite the prayer his parents had just gone over, he had already fallen asleep. And his parents both kissed him goodnight.

# Gary's Prayer

In today's world there is no better time to arm our children with the Word of God. Gary's prayer is a book that will aid children in learning how to talk to God at an early age while learning to develop a relationship with God.

# Amen!

Made in the USA
Middletown, DE
03 September 2023

37448729R00015